FAIRY TALES

WELL-KNOWN STORIES TO
READ AND SHARE

Written by Helen Anderton

Illustrated by Stuart Lynch

make
believe
ideas

CONTENTS

BEAUTY AND THE BEAST

Once, there was a prince called Wayne
who was selfish, mean, and vain.
"I hate to share!" he'd storm and shout,
"It's worse than eating Brussels sprouts!"

He had no friends – just lots of things
like toys and jewels and diamond rings.
But what Prince Wayne loved most of all
were roses from his castle wall.

Wayne's mean neighbor, Witchy Lou,
    secretly liked roses, too.
One day she tried to steal a stem,
    but Wayne cried, "Stop! You can't have them!"

The witch thought, "Wayne will pay for this!"
    She cried out in an angry hiss,
"An ugly, hairy beast you'll be
    until true love can set you free!"

She swished her wand six times (at least)
    and Wayne became a snarling beast!
He had black eyes and gruesome hair,
    and claws just like a grizzly bear!

From that day on life wasn't easy –
    the sight of Wayne made people queasy.
He soon forgot the witch's spell
    and gave up on true love as well.

Some years passed, 'til one cold day
   a girl called Beauty passed that way.
Her hair was tied back in a plait,
   beneath her favorite woolen hat.

She saw the roses, pink and red.
   "I think I'll pick one!" Beauty said.
But just as Beauty plucked a rose,
   the beast jumped out, and Beauty froze!

"LEAVE MY ROSES BE," Beast cried.
"Please don't eat me!" she replied.
Said Beast, "You took a rose for free –
to pay me back, stay here with me!"

16

The girl decided to be brave
    (the beast looked fairly well-behaved).
So she followed Beast inside –
    but what a sight then met her eyes!

In the hall, the walls were ripped;

the wooden floors were stained and chipped.

Beast looked sadly at his paws.

"I rip everything with these claws!"

20

"Poor Beast, I'll help you!" Beauty cried,
and went to find two sticks outside.
She pulled her woolen hat to bits,
and then the girl began to knit.

Soon Beauty joined the beast downstairs.
She said, "I've solved your rips and tears!"
She gently picked up Beast's four paws,
and put a mitten on each claw!

Beast was thrilled! He ran around,
gently padding on the ground.
Nothing scratched or ripped straight through –
his paws were safe, and toasty, too!

He plucked some roses off the wall
and said to Beauty, "Have them all!"
With a shock, young Beauty knew:
She loved him – and he loved her, too!

In a flash and with a BOOM,
the handsome prince was in the room.
Love had broken Lou's cruel spell,
and cured Wayne's selfishness as well!

25

The End

CINDERELLA

Once a girl called Cinderella
was locked up in a gloomy cellar
by Eve and Val, her jealous sisters
(next to her they looked like blisters).

Then one day an invitation
was sent to each home in the nation.
"Prince Billy is looking to be wed.
Come to the royal ball!" it said.

Invitation

"Huzzah!" yelled Cinders, "Just the fella
to free me from this gloomy cellar!"
Eve and Val declared, "Fat chance!
YOU'RE not going to the dance!"

They locked her up with ghastly grins,
and powdered both their slimy chins.
Then they left and Cinders wept,
but luckily, just then in stepped . . .

a zucchini fairy, full of cheer!

She said, "I'm here to help, my dear.

I'll get you to the ball in time,

with these zucchini tools of mine!"

She brought one out, quite long and green;
   it turned into a limousine!
Soon Cinders had a brand-new dress
   and two shoes – made of glass, no less!

"At midnight," said the fairy, "flee,
   or a zucchini you will be!"
So Cinders left in her new ride,
   with bright green soggy seats inside!

When Cinders got to Billy's dance,

she fell for him with just one glance.

The pair began to dance around,

while Eve and Val just watched and frowned.

But soon, the clock began to strike –

there was no time to say good-night!

Cinders ran, but in her haste

she left one shoe at Billy's place!

Billy vowed, "I'll search for you –
the girl who fits this tiny shoe!"
But though the prince went far and wide,
no girl could get her foot inside!

Some tried tape and some tried glue.
Some got angry at the shoe.
Some greased up their feet with soap –
one even tied her toes with rope!

Soon Billy got to Cinders' door,

but she was locked downstairs once more.

Eve and Val were there instead.

"Try this shoe!" Prince Billy said.

They each took turns, trying and yelling:

"It fits! IT FITS! Ignore the swelling!"

"Does no one else live here?" asked Billy.

They shook their heads. "No – don't be silly!"

Cinders knew what she should do.
She picked up glass shoe number two,
then smashed it on a heavy rock
and used the heel to pick the lock!

43

She ran upstairs and cried out, "Hey!
I'll try that shoe on, if I may!"
And without Cinders forcing it,
the shoe slipped on – a perfect fit!

The prince proposed; she was delighted!
 (Eve and Val were not invited.)
And though their feet got rather wet,
 in a ZUCCHINI, they were wed!

The End

HANSEL AND GRETEL

Crammed into a house,
with no room to spare,
lived Dad, Hansel, Gretel,
and their stepmother, Clare.

48

They all were so hungry,
with nothing to eat
except for brown bread –
their one special treat.

49

One day, Clare told Dad
what she would do:
"I'll go to the woods
and get rid of those two!"

She marched to the woods,
with the children behind.
But Gretel left breadcrumbs
for them to find.

Then Clare crept away
and they filled up with dread.
They looked for the crumbs
but found birds instead!

52

Poor Hansel cried out,
   "We'll both starve out here!"
He shivered and shook,
   and whimpered with fear.

But then, through the trees,
   they spied something sweet:
a gingerbread house
   all covered in treats!

They chomped at the roof
and chewed at the floor,
then munched on the chimney,
and wolfed down the door!

Then out came a witch
so ugly and green
that when Hansel saw her,
he let out a SCREAM!

"Oh, don't be a wimp!"
said Gretel in shock.
He said, "But she's gross –
she smells like a sock!"

"You've ruined my house!"
said the witch feeling sad.
"My face may be ugly,
but at least I'm not bad!"

"I spent my life baking;
it was my one dream
to live in a house
all covered in cream!"

The children felt guilty,
    for mean she was not.
As the witch ran inside,
    they worked up a plot . . .

They nibbled the roof
and chomped at the wall.
They guzzled and gulped
'til a castle stood tall!

Then out came the witch
and they worked as a team.
"It needs just one thing:
swirls of whipped cream!"

When it was finished,
the three made amends
and all lived together
in the castle as friends.

The End

LITTLE RED RIDING HOOD

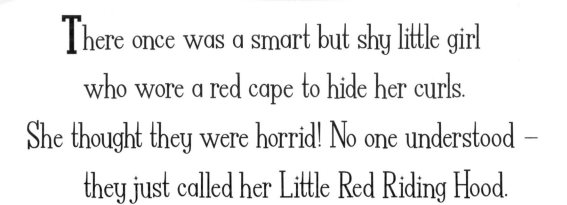

There once was a smart but shy little girl
who wore a red cape to hide her curls.
She thought they were horrid! No one understood –
they just called her Little Red Riding Hood.

69

Little Red's granny had been very sick.

　She needed some pills and a walking stick.

She lived in a cottage, deep in the wood,

　and she loved her Little Red Riding Hood.

Said Red to her mom, "Please let me see Gran."

　"Of course," Mom said. "What an excellent plan!"

Mom packed for Gran all the food she could,

　to be sent with Little Red Riding Hood.

Little Red's mom said, "Beware how you go.
Don't speak to strangers and don't dawdle so!"
Then over the gate and into the wood
skipped innocent Little Red Riding Hood.

74

But a nasty wolf had spied Little Red.

"Where are you going so quickly?" he said.

"To dear Granny's cottage, here in the wood,"

squeaked terrified Little Red Riding Hood.

Wolf dashed away with an idea in mind.

At Granny's cottage he knew what he'd find!

If his brilliant plan worked as it should,

soon he could EAT Little Red Riding Hood.

On tiptoes Wolf crept to Granny's front door
and went right in (hearing Granny's loud snore).

He swallowed her whole – because he could!
Then he waited for Little Red Riding Hood.

Red rang the bell when she reached Granny's home.

"Come in, dear," she heard (in Wolf's growly tone).

"Why, Granny, your eyes look bigger!" Red cried.

"The better to SEE you with," Wolf replied.

"And, Granny, your ears look bigger — and black!"

"The better to HEAR you with," Wolf said back.

"And, Granny, your teeth look much bigger, too!"

Roared Wolf, "All the better for ME to eat YOU!"

Wolf gobbled Red and his belly grew round!
Meanwhile a woodsman had tracked the wolf down . . .

He sliced the wolf open – there Granny stood,
and with her was Little Red Riding Hood!

From then on, the girl wasn't shy anymore
about showing the curls she had hated before.
She taught wolves manners and how to be good,
and threw out that silly red riding hood!

The End

THE PRINCESS AND THE PEA

To live a very happy life,
Prince Lee must find a royal wife.
But his mom, the queen, is tough –
no girl she meets is good enough!

Each day, the queen goes out to see
if she can find a match for Lee.
A girl must pass one hundred tests
to prove that she's a true princess.

"This girl has chewed her fingernails.
This one doesn't sing – she WAILS!
This girl hasn't brushed her teeth.
Goodness me! What smelly feet!"

"We need a princess," says the queen,
"who's pretty, fragile, sweet, and CLEAN!"
The prince says, "Yes, Mom, I agree,
these girls aren't good enough for me!"

That night, the pair get quite a shock
  when from the door, they hear a KNOCK!
They peep out through the windowpane
  and see a princess in the rain.

"She looks well-groomed, so let her in!"
shouts Prince Lee with an eager grin.
The girl says, "Hi, I'm Princess Dee.
Would you spare a bed for me?"

The prince says, "She's the best we've seen."
The queen says, "All right – she looks clean!
Let's put her through a few quick tests
to prove that she's a true princess!"

All dried out, the
girl looks great:

she has good manners;
she sits up straight;

each song she sings
is such a treat –

she even has
nice-smelling feet!

Prince Lee declares, "Dee is the one!"
"One last test, though!" says his mom.
"Eighty soft layers make the bed
upon which Dee will rest her head."

"Then underneath all of that fluff,
we'll put a pea that's strong enough
to bruise a princess who is true
and good enough to marry you!"

The next day, he goes in to see
what has happened to Princess Dee.
She whines, "I didn't get to snooze;
something gave me a big bruise!"

Prince Lee jumps and bellows, "Success!
You know, only a true princess
would be able to feel that pea,
so please, Dee, will you marry me?"

The queen is glad – she jumps with joy:
"I've found a princess for my boy!"
And with the pea on royal display,
the pair get married right away.

The End

PUSS IN BOOTS

A mean old miller died one day,
and written in his will,
he gave two sons the house and horse,
while the cat was left to Bill.

Bill asked his brothers, "Can't you help?"
(He was in a tricky spot.)
But they said, "Go! And take that cat,"
leaving Bill with not a lot.

Bill said, "Oh, what can I do?
Perhaps I'll eat my cat!"
But the crafty cat, on hearing this,
said, "Hey! Please don't do that!"

Said Puss, "Buy me a bag and boots –
I'll make your dreams come true.
Trust me, and I will bring you gold,
and a wife and a palace, too."

113

Thrilled, Bill found a bag and boots.
Then Puss said, "Here's the plan:
We'll take some gifts to please the king –
and make you a wealthy man."

Puss caught a rabbit in the bag,
and then he made a stew.
"I'll take this to the king," he said,
"and say it comes from you."

Puss gave many gifts this way –
delivering them by hand.
He told the king, "They're from Lord Stone!"
(To make young Bill sound grand.)

"Now," Puss said, "trust me once more.
Go take a morning swim."
And while Bill swam, Puss stole his clothes –
which put Bill in a spin!

Just then the royal coach came past,
    so Puss said with a grin,
"Sire, Lord Stone's been robbed by thieves!"
    Said the king to Bill, "Get in!"

The princess gave Bill smart new clothes,
    and to thank her for this kindness,
Puss said, "Sire, at Lord Stone's home
    we have a feast for you and Her Highness!"

Puss had one thing left to do.
He ran ahead to find
a palace lived in by a troll –
the mean and nasty kind.

This troll could change into a bee,
a lion, or a seal.
Puss thought, "If I can trick the troll,
his palace is mine to steal."

Said Puss, "Now, Troll, I hear it's true
you can be a lion or bee.
I picture you as a fierce beast,
but it's a MOUSE I'd like to see."

With that, the troll became a mouse –
right there on the floor!
In a flash, Puss ate him up
and wrote "Lord Stone" on the door.

Lord Stone

Lord
Stone

Puss stood proudly at the door
as the royal coach arrived.
The king was amazed and said to Bill:
"Take my daughter as your bride!"

127

Bill had all that he could want
with a palace and his wife.
And Puss in Boots was free to live
a long and happy life!

129

The End

RAPUNZEL

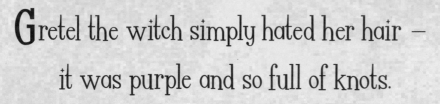

Gretel the witch simply hated her hair –
it was purple and so full of knots.
And what made it worse was living next door
to a girl who had long golden locks.

This girl, Rapunzel, had gold hair so long
that people would stop just to stare!
Gretel was jealous – she wanted a wig.
So she thought, "I'll steal that girl's hair!"

Now, Gretel liked to grow spinach and beans,

which Rapunzel's mom hungrily spied.

"Steal us some beans!" she cried to her husband,

who willingly ran right outside.

135

Just at that moment, he heard a great POP –
the witch appeared out of the blue!
"My prize vegetables! You will pay for this!
I'll chop you up into a stew!"

Said the dad (turning pale), "Please spare my life!"
Grinning, the witch said, "I might . . .
Give me your daughter, and I'll let you go."
Shaking, the dad said, "All right!"

Gretel was thrilled that the wig of her dreams
would soon be in her power!
"I'll wait for her hair to grow longer," she thought,
and locked the girl in a tower.

With no tower door, Rapunzel would wait
until three o'clock every day.
That was the hour when Gretel arrived,
and cleared her throat loudly to say:

"Ahoy up there, let down your hair!"

Rapunzel threw down her very long plait
and Gretel climbed up in a flash.

She took out a ruler and measured the hair,
then said with a smile, "I must dash!"

One day, Rapunzel felt so alone
    she started to sing a sad song.
As luck would have it, a charming young prince
    heard her as he walked along.

He circled the tower – where was the door?
    The walls were too high to climb!
But just at that moment, Gretel appeared
    and shouted her usual rhyme:

"Ahoy up there, let down your hair!"

"So that's how it's done!" he thought to himself.
And the next day, to Rapunzel's surprise,

instead of the witch, the charming young prince
appeared in front of her eyes!

The prince came to visit day after day
and everything was going fine,
'til one afternoon, when Gretel appeared
in the tower at just the same time!

Seeing the prince, she screamed out in rage,
   "Oi, you! Get away from that hair!"
She tried to push him out of the tower,
   but Rapunzel cried out, "Don't you dare!"

Quickly, Rapunzel cut off all her hair
and said (as glad as could be),

"Here, have my braid – I'll take the prince."
And with that, Rapunzel was free!

149

The pair were soon married (R. wore a hat).
And to show they had no hard feelings,
they invited the witch, who wore a wig
that was gold and reached to the ceiling!

151

The End

SNOW WHITE

Snow White lives with a pretty queen,
who's cruel, unkind, and just plain mean.
She talks to her mirror on the wall –
his name is Bill, and here's his call:

"You gorgeous queen, you're fair, you're great!

I'd love to take you on a date.

Says this mirror on the wall:

The queen is fairest of them all!"

The queen just loves to wake each day
and hear the things Bill has to say.
But then, one day, in sunny June,
Bill decides to change his tune:

"You gorgeous queen, you're fair, it's true,
but Snow White has grown more fair than you.
Says the mirror on the wall:
Snow White is fairest of them all!"

The queen is mad. She stomps, then screams,
"Snow, you've ruined all my dreams!"

"You're banished now; go on, GET OUT!"
So Snow White doesn't hang about.

Snow runs and runs – she's terrified!
She needs to find a place to hide.
Then seven dwarfs hop off a bus
and say, "Poor dear! Come live with us!"

Those dwarfs are such a happy bunch!
They let Snow stay and feed her lunch.
She tries to make their home looks nice.
She keeps it clean – and free of mice!

Back home, the queen works up a plot
and mixes poison in a pot.
She dips in apples, big and red.
"When Snow White bites one,

she'll be dead!"

Then, disguised in a cloak and hood,
the queen finds Snow White in the wood.

She gives her a red apple for lunch
and Snow falls down with the first crunch!

The dwarfs decide to place Snow White
inside a case. They watch each night,
so her fair face they can remember.
But then things change, for in September . . .

A prince sees Snow: "Wow, what a girl!
    Hair like ebony, skin like pearls –
I have to kiss her, stand aside!"
    One kiss, and Snow opens her eyes!

The queen thinks it is safe at last
    to talk to Bill now that Snow has passed.
"You gorgeous queen, you're fair, it's true,
    but Snow is still fairer than you!"

The queen replies, "I know you're wrong.
   You must be broken; Snow is gone!"
She throws Bill out the castle door
   and hears him crashing to the floor.

The queen is glad – she doesn't know
the fairest in the land is Snow.
Now, Snow White and the prince are free
to live together happily!

The End

THE UGLY DUCKLING

Mommy Duck has ten round eggs,
   all tucked up in her nest.
The eggs go CRACK! The ducklings hatch,
   but one's not like the rest.

This duckling isn't yellow
   but rather gray instead.
"He's not the same. He needs a name,"
   says Mom, "I'll call him Ned."

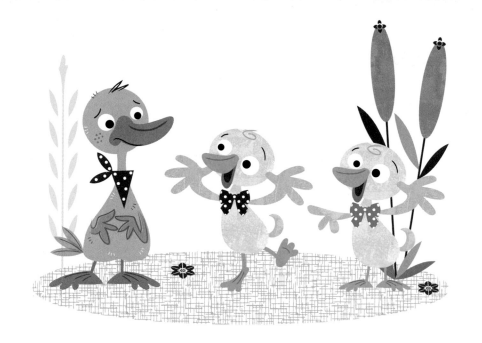

"Ned is ugly. Ned's so big!"

tease the duckling brothers.

Thinks Ned, "It's true.
What can I do?
I'm not like the others."

In the pond the ducklings learn
to swim in one neat line.

But with a SPLASH, poor Ned goes CRASH
right through the ducklings nine!

Then it's time to learn to QUACK,
    but Ned shouts, "HOOT!" with glee!
The ducklings laugh, and feeling daft,
    Ned sulks behind a tree.

"Hoot!"

QUACK!

Ned decides: "It's time to go –
  I'll find a different flock."
And off he roams, so far from home,
  with just his favorite sock.

First he asks some dancing geese,
"Please, can I join your team?"

184

The geese say, "No, you'll spoil our show.
But why not try upstream?"

185

Then Ned asks a magpie pair.

But on a sign they write:

×××××××××××
No ducks allowed —
and three's a crowd.
×××××××××××

Thinks Ned, "How impolite!"

As the moon and stars shine down,
Ned feels so out of luck.

A tear he weeps before he sleeps.
Poor Ned, the ugly duck.

He stays inside the sock for weeks.
Then one day, by surprise,
a noise wakes Ned, and from his bed,
an awesome sight he spies.

A group of birds so graceful,

with long, white necks that bend.

They welcome Ned with wings outspread,

and say, "Come, join us, Friend!"

Shyly, Ned swims to the birds
and asks, "How can this be?
For I'm so plain — please, do explain:
Just why would you pick me?"

"Look at your reflection, Ned!"
call the birds together.
And then he sees . . .

an orange beak,

a neck so sleek,

and beautiful WHITE feathers.

Ned's as happy as can be,
with somewhere to belong.
Says Ned, "I'm free just to be me:
no duck – I'm Ned the SWAN!"